Birthday

ALSO BY CÉSAR AIRA FROM NEW DIRECTIONS

———————

Conversations

Dinner

Ema, the Captive

An Episode in the Life of a Landscape Painter

Ghosts

The Hare

How I Became a Nun

The Linden Tree

The Literary Conference

The Little Buddhist Monk and *The Proof*

The Miracle Cures of Dr. Aira

The Musical Brain

The Seamstress and the Wind

Shantytown

Varamo

Birthday

•

CÉSAR AIRA

Translated by Chris Andrews

A NEW DIRECTIONS PAPERBOOK ORIGINAL

Originally published by Random House Mondadori, Barcelona, as *Cumpleaños* in 2001;
published in conjunction with the Literary Agency Michael Gaeb/Berlin

This work is published with the help of the "Sur" Translation Support Program of the
Ministry of Foreign Affairs and Culture of the Argentine Republic.
*Obra editada en el marco del Programa "Sur" de Apoyo a las Traducciones del Ministerio de
Relaciones Exteriores y Culto de la República Argentina.*

Manufactured in the United States of America
First published as a New Directions Paperbook (NDP1435) in 2019
New Directions books are published on acid-free paper
Design by Erik Rieselbach

Library of Congress Cataloging-in-Publication Data
Names: Aira, César, 1949– author. | Andrews, Chris, 1962– translator.
Title: Birthday / César Aira ; translated from the Spanish by Chris Andrews.
Other titles: Cumpleaños. English
Description: New York, New York : New Directions Publishing Corporation, 2019. |
Originally published in Spain as Cumpleaños by Random House Mondadori.
Identifiers: LCCN 2018039770 | ISBN 9780811219099 (alk. paper)
Subjects: LCSH: Aira, César, 1949– | Authors, Argentine—20th century—Biography.
Classification: LCC PQ7798.1.17 Z46 2019 | DDC 868/.6403 [B]—dc23
LC record available at https://lccn.loc.gov/2018039770

10 9 8 7 6 5 4 3 2 1

New Directions Books are published for James Laughlin
by New Directions Publishing Corporation
80 Eighth Avenue, New York 10011

BIRTHDAY

I

RECENTLY I TURNED FIFTY, AND IN THE LEADSUP TO the big day I began to have great expectations, but not because I was really hoping to take stock of my life up to that point; I saw it more as a chance for renewal, a fresh start, a change of habits. In fact, I didn't even consider taking stock, or weighing up the half century gone by. My gaze was fixed on the future. I was thinking of the birthday exclusively as a point of departure, and although I hadn't worked out anything in detail or made any concrete plans, I had very bright hopes, if not of starting over entirely, at least of using that milestone to shed some of my old defects, the worst of which is precisely procrastination, the way I keep breaking my promises to change. It wasn't so preposterous. After all, it was entirely up to me. It was more reasonable than the hopes and fears pinned on the year 2000, because turning fifty is less arbitrary than a date in the almanac. In a reversal of the usual scenario, the hopes, however poorly grounded, were working in my favor, because they could sustain a self-fulfilling prophecy. And everything suggested that they would, or so I felt.

And yet nothing happened. My birthday came and went. The tasks to be completed, the chores to be done and the force of routine—which is so powerful by the age of fifty—vied with each other to ensure that the day went by like any other. It was my fault, of course: if I wanted there to be a change, I should have made it happen myself, but instead I trusted to the magic of the event, I took it easy and went on being the same old me. What else could I expect, in practical terms, if I had no intention of getting divorced, or moving house, or starting a new job, or doing anything special? In the end, I took it philosophically and went on living, which is no mean feat.

The mistake, if there was one, lay in not realizing that changes come from the most unexpected directions, which is what makes them genuine changes. It's a fundamental law of reality. What changes is something else, not what you were expecting. Otherwise, it would be business as usual. It's not really a failure of planning or foresight, or even a lack of imagination, because even imagination has its limits. Expectations of change develop around a particular subject, but change always changes the subject. I should have known that from my experience as a novelist. But I had to wait for events to bring it home to me.

A few months later, one beautiful autumn morning, I was walking along the street with Liliana. I looked up, breathing the cold, bracing air. The sky was clear, a luminous blue; up there, to my left, the moon, half-full, with that porous white color it has in the daylight; to the right, hidden from us by the buildings, the sun, still low. I was feeling euphoric, not unusually (it's

my natural state): buoyant and optimistic. I was chatting away
about something, and then, with the vague intention of crack-
ing some kind of joke, I said:

"It can't be true that the phases of the moon are produced by
the earth's shadow when it comes between the moon and the
sun, because the sun and the moon are both in the sky now, the
earth isn't between them at all, but the moon isn't full. They've
been fooling us! Hehehe. The phases of the moon must be
caused by something else, and they're telling us it's the shadow
of the earth! Hehe. It's garbage!"

My wife, who doesn't always appreciate my sense of humor,
looked up too, in puzzlement, and asked me:

"But who said the phases of the moon were caused by the
earth's shadow? Where did you get that from?"

"That's what I was taught in Pringles," I said, lying.

"It can't be. No one could have come up with that sort of
nonsense."

"But how does it work then?"

"There's no shadow. The sun illuminates the moon, but only
half of it, the way it is with any light source illuminating a spher-
ical body. Depending on the relative position of the earth, we
see a portion of the illuminated half; it grows until we're seeing
it all, and that's when there's a full moon; then it shrinks down
to nothing. Simple."

"Are you serious? So I was the only one getting it wrong all
this time? Hehe!"

We left it there, in a comic haze, one of the many I generate in the course of a day. All you have to do is say it's a "bad" joke, and no one bothers to look for its meaning. Except that I didn't forget this "joke," and little by little the monstrosity of my ignorance dawned on me. I had indeed been getting it wrong, and it wasn't as if, in this case, "it" was something obscure that anyone might be excused for misunderstanding. On the contrary, "it" was almost the model of the obvious and the visible. The fact that I considered myself an intellectual, an educated, curious, intelligent man, made the joke all the funnier. The moon is always suspended there in full view, lit up and conspicuous, each and every night, punctually running through the cycle of its phases twelve times a year. And the sun like a spotlight and the earth with its days and nights, the whole rotating system . . . Any eight-year-old with a modicum of intelligence could have reached the correct conclusions. Or a savage, a primitive, the first man making a first attempt at thought.

Preposterous as it may seem, there is a simple explanation for my ignorance on this point of basic cosmology: distraction. A historical moment of distraction. At some point in my childhood, I must have come up with that explanation of the moon's phases, perhaps in passing, without really thinking, using the narrow crescent of my brain that happened to be illuminated by my attention, and in all the years since then (almost fifty of them!) I had never given it another moment's thought. It wasn't a case of 'I never thought about it'; I thought about it *once*, which is worse.

It's ironic, because I was always being told that I was miles away, "on the moon." If that had been literally true, I'd have been none the wiser, because the earth, seen from there, would have similar phases, and for the same reason. Although on the moon (and this was something I did think about), I wouldn't have survived for more than half a minute, because of the lack of air. I wouldn't have had the time or the peace of mind to invent crazy stories about the heavenly bodies. The fear of suffocation, which has haunted every minute of my life, would have given me an excuse for not thinking. Meanwhile, I was on the earth, breathing perfectly, but the excuse remained. All I managed to come up with in a whole half century was a blank, a gap. The worst thing was knowing that my thought could have been full of gaps like that.

My only miserable consolation was to think that these moments of distraction were the price that I had paid for attending to other questions, that economizing mental activity in one area had allowed me to concentrate more lucidly in others. As an excuse, it's flimsy, but perhaps there's a thread of truth in it. Flimsy because the blind spot is so outrageous; but the truth might lie precisely in the exorbitance of the price. Maybe I had ignored too much in order to give myself the latitude for invention that I needed to cover up my ignorance in other areas. Since I didn't even know how to live, it would have been a scandalous waste of my modest capacities to devote them to understanding something as useless and decorative as the phases of the moon. The sole and ultimate aim of all my work has been to compensate for my incapacity to live, and the work has barely sufficed to keep me afloat. I have done a lot, but only just enough. Is it really so surprising that I've had to pay for my survival with scandalous gaps? To reach the age of fifty, a man with my abysmal defects would have to be a genius, and since I'm not, I've had to pretend, constructing a laborious and complicated simulation, which was bound to produce an unbalanced figure, with dramatic highs and lows in all the wrong places, that is, the silhouette of a monster.

This business with the moon has got me thinking. As I said, what bothers me is not so much that I was mistaken about what makes the moon wax and wane; it's the way I came up with a hasty and fallacious explanation and never gave it another thought. This must have happened at some point in my childhood. But when, exactly? On what day? At what time? In what circumstances? It would seem impossible to pinpoint. That faraway past is an inextricable blend of forgetting and invention, from which stray fragments emerge by chance. If I try to remember thinking about the moon, the only thing that comes back to me is the memory of a summer night in Pringles: I would have been seven or eight; we had gone out onto the sidewalk after dinner, as usual, and I was playing with Omar, one of the neighborhood kids, while our parents chatted. Omar and I were inseparable; we were the same age, and he lived next door. The nights in Pringles were very dark: there were just a few weak street lamps suspended over the corners, and only where the streets were paved; since ours was the last street with asphalt on

that side of town, the great darkness stretched away behind us.
Also, the houses were scantly lit. Electricity was still a new and
strange technology for us, and the expense of it was a source
of worry; no bulb was ever left on, not even for a minute, unless it was being used. When we went out onto the sidewalk
for some fresh air after dinner, we were careful to switch off all
the lights in the house. These conditions favored the contem-
plation of the starry vault, which shone as I have never seen it
shine anywhere else. The Milky Way ran in the same direction
as our street. Looking up at the moon that night, Omar said:
"The moon is good, don't you think?" Good? It seemed the least
appropriate adjective. Why good? Because it always kept him
company, wherever he went. "Look," he said, "See it there?" It
was to our left and a bit behind us, as if peering over our shoul-
ders. Omar ran off as fast as he could, and I followed him. After
thirty yards, he stopped: "There it is, in the same place." Sure
enough, it was still on our left and a bit behind, as if it had run
along with us. Omar explained this idea of his as something that
he had believed 'when he was a kid,' that is, in some distant past,
although he wasn't even ten. I have noticed that children often
measure their brief lives in this way, as if they were eternities.
He was probably being ironic too — it wouldn't have been unusual — and I guessed that there was something going on from
the way he was looking at me a little too insistently. Perhaps he
was setting some kind of trap; we were engaged in a constant
battle of wits (this too is fairly common among children). I must

have quickly reassessed the possibilities in play, because I connected this moon game with another memory (unless I'm making the connection now).

Once I had gone with my parents to a furniture store in town, the biggest or maybe the only one. It would have been to buy something, but I can't remember what. At some point my parents got into a conversation with the owner's wife, a fat lady of a certain age, very smartly dressed, with a bouffant, a pearl necklace and a thick Italian accent. I think the store had just opened, and the lady was singing its praises and pointing out its charms. She showed us a picture hanging on the wall; it was a portrait, of a woman, I think, though not of anyone in particular, no doubt a cheap reproduction, but the lady said that there was something very special about it: if you stood right in front of the picture, the eyes of the model looked straight into yours … But if you took a few steps to the side (she invited us to see for ourselves), the painted woman's eyes continued to return your gaze. Wherever you went, the picture was always looking back at you; it was like a magic trick. The lady laughed contentedly and repeated that it was a very special, very ingenious picture. I should add that the painting was for decoration, not for sale, so this was not a pitch, and the lady didn't actually work at the store, she just went there to keep her husband company and chat with the customers, out of sheer boredom, like so many of the storekeeper's wives in town. Her praise was sincere. My parents expressed polite admiration, and I spent all the rest of the visit in front of the picture, moving to the side, coming up close, stepping back. When we left, my mother laughed at the lady's ignorance: what she had taken for a unique and marvelous feature was common to every picture or photograph in which the model had been looking directly at the painter or the camera. I agreed, but whether it was something I already knew or had just learned, I honestly couldn't have said.

I had the feeling that something similar lay behind Omar's remark about the moon. Likely as not, he was trying to get me to lower my guard and confess that there was an aspect of the world whose workings I didn't understand. Children are always testing each other like that, setting up complicated charades to extract involuntary confessions of ignorance. When they come across an adult who is ignorant in some way, like the lady in the furniture store, that person serves as a milestone in the child's learning about life.

In any case, the two phenomena are quite different: the painting's fixed yet mobile gaze on one hand and the phases of the moon on the other. And yet by using associations to bridge the gap, perhaps I could pinpoint the moment at which I made the error, triangulating it with two boys setting traps for each other, and myself at fifty in the role of the transtemporal adult with a particular gap in his knowledge. But I really can't be bothered. It would take too long; and there would be no guarantee of success.

The past is not an imaginary construction like any other. I don't know how some people—modern historians, for example—can say that it is. What happened happened precisely because it was real. The details of the past are of capital importance, not only for establishing a chronology but also because of the interplay of causes and effects. Although the present is overdetermined, it is attached by subtle threads to some atom of reality, which can only be identified by locating it precisely in the series of past events.

Everything that I have written so far leads me to suppose that my incapacity to live has its origin in the moment at which I made my error, or failed to pay attention, or came up with my hasty explanation of the phases of the moon. So if I were able to reconstruct the history of that instant, I would solve the mystery that has always haunted me.

It would be less dramatic, but much more plausible, to say that it wasn't a moment but a process: the process of wasting time, which is long by its very nature. At my age, it's impossible to contemplate the eternities of time that I wasted in my youth without a certain horror. The lack of method, the capricious detours, the waiting for nothing. The hours, the days, the years, the decades squandered. And it is poetically just, in a way, that the apparent victim should have been the moon, that poetic reminder of wasted time.

II

TODAY I CAME TO PRINGLES, FOR A WEEK. I WROTE THE
previous chapter this morning, in the Café del Avenida, which
was completely empty, as the cafés here usually are, under the
watchful eye of the waitress. She's young and new to the café,
or new to me at least (I come here two or three times a year).
When she served me, she asked if I was a writer, and declared
the high regard in which she holds that occupation. She writes
too, she told me, all the time, whenever she can, to get things
off her chest, to express herself, etc. To judge from her haste
to tell me this, I was the first writer she had met, and she was
excited by the idea of being able to talk, at last, with someone
in the trade. She kept watching me all through my session of
writing, partly because she had nothing else to do, and when I
went to pay at the counter she brought up the subject again. She
wanted me to tell her what it's like to be a writer, but in the end
(it's always the way) she did most of the talking. What follows
is a summary of what she told me.

She is seventeen years old and comes from Suárez; she's
only in Pringles because she got a job here. On her days off she

goes back to Suárez, where her parents and brothers live. She's not studying. She's very blonde, very white, tall and extremely slim, not pretty but fresh and eager. She must belong to one of the numerous communities of so-called "Russians" in Suárez. They call themselves "Germans," and curiously they're both, as I understand: "Volga Germans," that is, Germans who immigrated to Russia during the time of Catherine the Great and Potemkin, or something like that; I ought to know, because I'm descended from them too.

She writes. She's always writing, she couldn't live without it. She can put in writing what she couldn't say out loud. One time she got the second prize in an essay competition, with a "Letter to Jesus." I asked her if the theme was set or if she had chosen it herself. It took her a very long time to understand what I was asking. It was her choice. She felt that people, especially the young, were neglecting Jesus. They only remember Jesus when they need him, when things go wrong, and the rest of the time they forget him. There was nothing I could say to that.

For her, writing is the only way to express and understand what is happening to her. At this point I asked her how old she was. "A lot has happened in my life," she said. The main thing is that now she has overcome the fear of death, which obsessed her for many years. Now she has realized that death is not the end, that after this life, there is another, like this one or better, because there's no pain. She learned this from the death of her older brother, who was the most important person in her life. Her brother was a father to her, the father she didn't have because her real father walked out when she was little and never came back. Her brother was always there for her, whenever she needed him, helping her even before she had asked him for his help. And even though he's dead now, he's still there for her. Sometimes she finds herself talking to him, sometimes she can sense that someone is there beside her, and it's her brother. For her, this supernatural accompaniment is linked to the experience of writing. And it's the source of her conviction that there is another life: her brother is still alive in some way, free of the pain that was all he knew in this life. I wasn't saying much, just nodding and asking a question every now and then, but later on it occurred to me that she was contradicting herself, because what the accompaniment showed was that her brother hadn't gone off to live another life (like her father), but had stayed in this one, doing what he did for her when he was alive, except that he had been relieved of his wretched material form.

After these confidences, delivered so naturally, as if her whole life was made of nothing else, as if speaking and confiding were the same, she returned without missing a beat to her habit: she's always writing, especially going home on the bus. The last time, for example, just as she was about to arrive, something occurred to her, and she had to scribble it down in a hurry before the bus came to a stop, because she was afraid she might forget it otherwise. There I was able to add my two cents' worth: the same thing happens to me; I'm always noting down my ideas because if I don't, I forget them; they disappear completely, especially the ideas in my mind at the moment of waking, which are the most fugitive because there's no way to reconstruct the chain of thoughts that led to them. I've kicked myself so many times for not having noted them down! Later I remember having had an excellent idea, but I can't remember what it was and I agonize over that empty, definitively empty promise. She stood there in silence, with a blank look, as if to say, "How strange." We were talking about two different things.

Her hands were red, no doubt from all the washing of glasses and cups that she has to do at the café. Pretty teeth. Underneath her childlike confidence, there was a kind of anxiety that was hard to pin down. I made some remark about writing as a secret, for something to say more than anything else, but she didn't react: it clearly wasn't a secret for her. I had been thinking of myself at her age: secrecy and writing were almost synonymous. Maybe she didn't have any secrets. Or just the two that she had already told me: the fear of death, which she had overcome, and her habit of noting down ideas. I pictured her in the context of her community: the harsh climate, the devout faith, the ignorance, the poverty, the tradition of endogamy that had made her so blonde and confident, and possibly killed her brother, who may have been ill from birth and had survived and suffered for twenty years. Her brother was Jesus, dead and risen, and she was his evangelist.

There was something I really wanted to ask her, but I was too embarrassed: what kind of notebook did she use for noting down her ideas on the fly, for example in the bus? It's a question I would like to ask all writers, in the hope that statistics might help me approach my dream of a notebook adapted to all circumstances.

There was another important point that we didn't go into: the ideas that are there in your mind when you wake up. That must have been what she was noting down in the bus. She would have fallen asleep during the trip, the way young people do when they travel. Otherwise she wouldn't have told me specifically that it happened as the bus was coming into her town. Habit's internal clock had woken her on arrival, and there it was, the idea that she wanted to record. That's when ideas come to me too, although of course at my age I sleep much less. But this is more than balanced by all the sleeping I've done in fifty years. I attach a special importance to those waking ideas, not because they rise from some oneiric or unconscious depth (I don't believe in such things), but because of the position they occupy, on the far side of an absence. You have left the world, for a long or short span of time ... and then you return. On returning, you find the world where you left it but slightly altered by the action of time (even if you were only gone for a minute).

Or a tenth of a second, the blink of an eye. Things move very quickly in these absences. Even if there were notebooks and pens that made it possible to keep up with thought, the leap between the departure and the return would still elude them.

I am not an adept of Jesus, but I can imagine more or less how his historical nature works on believers. He gave our civilization the Past. Death and resurrection made him the god of the leap, the model for the functioning of gaps in time. A long-standing fear of death can prepare the way for his teaching.

The girl at the Avenida came to the conclusion that there is no reason to fear death. She learned this from the habit of writing (the secret that is not a secret) and the ideas that come out of the blue and have to be noted down. Personally, I think there's something much more frightening than individual death, and that's the death of everyone, the death of the world that we know and are, in other words, the End of the World. Paradoxically, we don't have to wait until we die as individuals to experience that great death, because the End of the World is with us every day; it is occurring imperceptibly in every little thing that happens, in the randomness of acts and thoughts.

III

MY MAIN FAULT, AND THE ROOT OF ALL THE OTHERS, IS
the lack of a stable and predictable rhythm in which acts and
ideas would find their places one after another. If I had such a
rhythm, it wouldn't matter if there were gaps here and there, because they would fill themselves. It would even be gratifying to
have specific gaps in my knowledge or experience: I would have
the satisfaction of seeing them closed as a matter of course by
the natural progression of my existence (it would make me feel
that life, with all its lessons, is worth living).

My style is irregular: scatterbrained, spasmodic, jokey—
necessarily jokey because I have to justify the unjustifiable by
saying that I didn't mean it seriously. But if necessity intervenes,
it's no joke. I wasn't really joking when I made that stupid quip
about the moon. And of course it didn't fool anyone. The gaps
go on being gaps forever, unless some wildly improbable circumstance happens to correct me. If they were only gaps in
knowledge, I wouldn't be so worried; but there are gaps in experience too, and again they can only be plugged by serendip-
ity. The numbers in this game of chance are so enormous that

just thinking about them makes me dizzy. What can I hope for, realistically, if all the objective conditions required for such an event line up once in a million years?

This lack of a regular rhythm explains why I have to note down each idea that occurs to me. My ideas are as slight and fleeting as seconds in the totality of time and so incoherent that I lose them if I don't make a note, because there's no connecting thread that I could follow back through all my distractions to recover them.

For the same reason, my mind is in continuous movement, flittering restlessly. Making a note of everything is beyond the bounds of human possibility. One thing I have idly fantasized about is inventing a notepad capable of capturing the hyperactivity of the brain. That must be the source of my fetishistic attachment to stationery and pens. I really should use some kind of shorthand, but I manage more or less with normal writing. In the end, all these daydreams about being the designer of one's own peculiarities are futile because they are just metaphors for what ends up happening anyway: I became a writer and my little novels fulfil the roles of magic notepad and shorthand.

But every writer would like to be a different sort of writer. That is what makes for the greatness and variety of literature. I would like to have style; if I did, all my experiences would be connected; my acts and thoughts would follow one another for a reason, not just by chance or on a whim. If there had been stable reasons underlying my behavior, I would have been spared

the kind of surprise the moon kept in store for me. I wouldn't
have needed to skip the basics; I would have covered them me-
thodically, in the proper sequence, and now I wouldn't be re-
gretting the time I wasted in my youth. Leaps are unnatural.
Time doesn't leap. To employ an imperfect but eloquent sim-
ile, my intellectual itinerary should have been like the prose of
those good eighteenth-century writers I have always tried to
take as my models. Each sentence contains an implicit question, to which the next sentence responds while posing a new
question ... Which means that everything is connected, and
it's almost impossible for the reader to get lost, because even
scant attention is stimulated and guided by a text put together
in that way.

Like so many before me, I made a virtue of necessity, and
turned my lack of style into a style. The concept of style, like
the concept of time, is a continuum that takes in everything,
including its own negations. This is how I came to be a well-
known and celebrated writer. I couldn't have done it any other
way; if I had tried to be like the others, there would have been
too much competition, and almost all of them would have been
better at it than me. But literature is wonderfully hospitable,
even beyond its own bounds, and that's why I'm so grateful to
it. That's why I have clung to literature in such a fanatical and
desperate way. Success never mattered to me ... That's what
everyone says, and usually it's not true. Success did actually
matter quite a lot to me, but only to provide a justification in

the eyes of society and my family, and allow me to go on writing. Otherwise I would have had to do it in secret, which would have been depressing.

I found life outside literature extremely difficult, so I left hardly anything outside. And yet, there's a sense in which everything is outside, from the moment I wake up till I go to bed, because I have to live like everyone else. The inside and the outside (of literature) are locked in a permanent struggle for supremacy; but rather than two armies clashing, they're like fluctuating forces, transforming and consuming each other. The disadvantages and problems and anxieties and paralysis that enter into literature, transformed into happiness machines, leave innumerable offspring behind (outside), which demand the same treatment ... As the years go by, stranger and more elaborate inventions are required; luckily it keeps getting easier, and History helps me out here too because it gives the impression that I'm developing, deepening my inner world ... I've often wondered how normal people occupy their time, because the work of staying alive takes up all the time I have, down to the last minute, and it's barely enough.

From my position as a Writer, I could regard the girl at the Avenida and her amateur's aspirations with a certain paternalistic superiority. That would be normal; it's what she would expect. But I feel that the time has come to see this question in a different light. Some time ago I began to feel that the young really can have superior aptitudes, in very rare, exceptional cases, one in a thousand, say ... But once you have granted the reality of a single case, it can be multiplied by any number you like. For some reason, I had never believed, until recently, in the real existence of prodigies; no doubt it was a defensive strategy, or a way of keeping my skepticism intact, in a single, solid block. I recognized them as a kind of poetic or didactic fiction; I thought that, like alien sightings, they could be explained by natural causes. But then, because of their very inconceivability, I began to accept them. This might be an effect of age: you start to see young people from the outside, as an aesthetic phenomenon, and they become strange, acquiring an objective weight and an opacity that could hide anything.

Since that grand fiasco with the moon, my embryonic belief has grown. I can extend it from public to private prodigies, and from there to humanity in general. For some reason, I was always surrounded, in my youth, by pedants, know-it-alls and loudmouths, who were always ready to set me straight. I responded with a hostile silence, which allowed me to preserve my mental integrity but also obliged me not to believe a word of what I heard. What if one of those people had taken it into his head to explain the phases of the moon to me? I would have thought him impolite; and this might begin to explain why I attach so much importance to good manners. In any case, those people must have known the real explanation. Who doesn't? And having that knowledge means taking a dizzying plunge into the past, casting your mind back many years to a youth lived in reality, in all its beauty: the youth of the world and the individual. Such things are learned at the appointed time, or never learned at all.

These last two days I have come to the Avenida to write, and the blonde girl hasn't been here. I have to call her the blonde girl because I don't know her name; I meant to ask her. When you have an inner life as busy as mine, it's awkward not to know the names of the characters who populate it; you have to make do with periphrases and nicknames, which seems impolite. Even the most casual relationships should begin like *Moby Dick*. I could ask the others, but I'd rather not. Today the waitress is another blonde girl, who (thankfully) is showing no interest in what I'm doing and seems more conventional. I wouldn't be surprised if the first girl had found another job, or moved, or got married; perhaps the day we talked was her last day in Pringles, and that detail (which she didn't disclose) was the key to everything she said. People have a way of disappearing suddenly from my life: I'm used to it. Life is change and movement. I stay still, doing the same thing every day, while everyone else is rushing around at a phenomenal speed.

The moon also participates in this logic of prodigious gifts. Except for the lack of intention or planning, its play with forms has all the subtle and ingenious precision of a bright young thing with no time to waste. Who will invent the moon's "magic notepad"? All of reality is like this.

IV

I HAVE TO SAY THAT THE WEATHER RIGHT NOW IN Pringles is horribly cold. Polar winds are blowing; the sun is a livid spot among the clouds; the roofs that I can see from my mother's apartment on the fifth floor of this uncommonly tall building are a uniform icy grey. The streets are empty all day, emptier than usual; and at night it's utterly desolate. There's something inhuman about this climate; it makes me think of vast interstellar spaces. The only things traversing the spaces outside are cars, driving slowly over the blue paving stones, whose gentle irregularity pummels their tires, making a distinctive, "Pringlish," murmuring sound that some people claim they could recognize among all the similar sounds produced by the cities of the world. It seems that even the cars are staying home unless they absolutely have to go out: they're following their usual routes, turning where they always turn, braking and accelerating in the same places. They have their own memory. They pass, and the street is empty again, not an atom moving.

Except for my daily stint of writing in the cafe, I'm spending the days in my room, lying on the bed and reading. I read one book after another, two a day if they're not too long, and if they're really bad (though none of them are), I speed up in the final chapters, skipping pages: I never give up before the end—a superstition that I really ought to shed. I get my books from the Municipal Library, which is just nearby, less than a hundred yards away. I go there first thing in the morning, spend a good while rummaging around, then choose something at random, without any plan or purpose, allowing myself to be guided by whims or momentary desires. Here in Pringles, with this inexhaustible library at my disposal, I read books that I would never have chosen otherwise, books that don't fit into any of the numerous reading projects that I'm constantly undertaking.

Yesterday, I read a short novel by Wells, *Una historia de los tiempos por venir,* literally *A History of the Times to Come,* which is a beautiful title, although I don't know what it was originally in English; the title page doesn't say, nor does it give the translator's name, or the date of publication, but I'm guessing it's from before 1900, one of the author's early works. (I know there's a book from the 1930s called *The Shape of Things to Come,* but I think that's a different one). It was one of the little volumes in the Biblioteca de La Nación series and it included "The Plattner Story" and some others. I borrowed the book for that story in particular (which turned out to be pretty slight), because I thought I could remember Borges mentioning it somewhere. I read the little novel about "the times to come" with pleasure, although it's not much good. As I was reading, I realized that what was really stimulating my interest (and this, I admit, is rather puerile) was finding the errors that the author had made in imagining what the world would be like in two hundred years' time. We're halfway there, and it's already obvious that he got it all wrong. Half the time, he stopped short, failing to imagine, for example, that technology would advance beyond the phonograph and the light bulb, and half the time he miscalculated the directions that progress would take. Wells is not the only one: all those who came after him were just as mistaken, if not more; and there's something peculiarly unfair about gloating over these errors, because the inescapable conclusion is that if we tried to do the same thing, we'd get it wrong too. The times to come are very slippery, very treacherous. But that extrapolation is just what makes the book interesting to read. Even after comprehending and overcoming the feeling of unjustified superiority that we get from noting the author's errors, we tend to think that we would not be so spectacularly wrong: after all, we can learn from the errors that Wells and all the others made. But no. The shot would still go wide of the mark; the mistakes would be even cruder. No real learning is possible in this area, because learning is done over time, but here time is the object. The title itself says it all, in a way: it's a "history" of the times to come, that is, of the future as realized and converted into materials for a narrative. Learning from the errors of others wouldn't work, because the will to learn would convert them into your own.

Wells makes a gross error when he assumes that in the twenty-second century women will still be submitting to their

husbands, unmarried girls will still be accompanied by chap-
erones, and so on. When it's just a matter of projecting on the
basis of a quantitative trend, it's easy. So Wells imagines more
populous cities, faster vehicles, taller buildings. But it doesn't
even occur to him that men might go out into the street without hats or sticks. Some things are unthinkable, and we don't
know what they are. Whatever the conditions that shape our
thought, those conditions exist, and there is, by definition, no
way to think outside them. This is the historical equivalent of
"changing the subject" in everyday life.

A perfectly easy and effective way of changing the subject is
to change books: you finish one, you start another. How many
books have I read in my life? I've lost count. It never occurred
to me to make lists or keep a running total, but I realize now
that I have always considered books in what could be called a
quantitative light. It must be because, as discrete and tangible
objects, they gave me a handle on the changing of the subject,
making it countable from a certain point of view (although
I never actually counted them). In a conversation, or in the
course of a morning, thought twists and turns, flowing almost
indivisibly, while books begin and end, and make up a clear
and obvious series.

I subscribe to the unoriginal theory that what makes a person unique and different from everyone else is a sum of particular experiences accumulated over the course of an existence.
This is what makes each person precious and irreplaceable, as
Nero implied when he said: "What a great artist the world is

losing." I don't know why people have been so hard on him.
Reading a book is, of course, an experience too, and the sum
of books that a person has read makes him or her unique as a
reader. One personal "library" is never quite the same as another. I suppose it *could* be, by an unlikely coincidence, if it
contained just a few, predictable titles; but with each new book
that is read, the probability of a match diminishes exponen-
tially. And I'm safe, because I have read a great deal, in several
languages, ranging over many ancient and modern literatures.
Although I can't claim to have set out to do this, it's as if my
eagerness to go on reading, at random, indiscriminately, one
book after another, good and bad, was a way of ensuring that
the "sum" finally produced by my experience as a reader would
be absolutely unique and without equal. That uniqueness, on
its own, ought to make me precious and irreplaceable, and give
me the equivalent of superpowers, or one at least, of a highly
specialized kind: something that no one else can do; and that's
enough for me.

But this reasoning doesn't really make much sense. If the
idea is to obtain a certain "sum" and make myself unique (so
that there will be a reason to lament my annihilation), there's
no need for thousands of books. Or anything, really, because
that sum is automatically produced by the elementary combi-
nation of four or five givens, which made me unique right from
the start. Child of W and X, born in place Y on day Z: that's all
you need. Of course this is the basic sum and not worth much,
because every last blade of grass has one. But there are other

sums, progressively acquired by work or luck, like decorations. They are all particularities, and for as long as I live, each moment of my existence will shower them upon me, countless and varied.

Not that they are necessarily virtuous, as the decoration metaphor might suggest. In fact, the most obvious individualizers are almost always defects: tics, bad habits, vices, transgressions. But they can also be odd gaps in knowledge. How many distinguished fifty-year-old writers could there be who don't know what makes the moon wax and wane? To accentuate the positive, it might be supposed that the bad exists for a good reason and without it things would be worse overall. The inexistence of anything, even crime, is an impoverishment. "Everything in life, even the performance of an autopsy, ends up producing some effect" (O. Lamborghini). Actually, I believe that the bad is more fertile than the good, because the good tends to produce satisfaction and complacency, while the bad generates uneasiness, which leads to the renewal of action. Action produces further errors, and the spiral of particularity spins off into the infinite. We all aspire to goodness, but because of the very conditions under which judgments of goodness are made, good people tend to resemble one another, and going too far in that direction would transform humanity into an undifferentiated and inert mass.

Action, the daughter of negativity, turns the "sum" back on itself. There is a kind of payment, a "refunding of the sum." To become unique and distinct is to prepare a testimony, for which our civilization has invented an ideal vehicle: art. Artists tend to be eccentric people, but I don't think it's because art has made them strange; rather their strangeness has led them to art. Or perhaps there is a reciprocal effect. In any case, this dialectic of debit and credit sums could resolve the fascinating aporias of Life and Work. Searching for the new and the strange in art is not the narcissistic task it might at first appear to be, because, for a start, it's not a matter of searching but of having found.

Of course, things don't always turn out as intended; if they did, all works would be masterpieces, and artists would always be young. To demonstrate this, it would suffice to compare the two images of my personal sum: what I would like to be and what I am.

V

ONE OF MY FRUSTRATED ASPIRATIONS IS TO DRESS IM-
peccably. It's something I have never achieved or even approx-
imated. I have always been messy, awkward, inelegant: too
warmly dressed in summer, shivering in winter.

It's one of the many things I keep putting off for when I get
rich; not that I expect to, on the contrary.

Everything I said before about the sum was based on the
mistaken postulation of a static figure, without taking the
movement of History into account. The sum is in flux, never
fixed. That's why you can never capitalize on it; in other words,
it's no use, except as a simulacrum. Actually, nothing is any use.
You can read thousands of books and go on being ignorant, as
I proved conclusively with my gaffe about the moon. To plug
that humiliating gap in my thought, I would have had to read,
in addition to all the other books, one specifically about the
visible forms of our poetic satellite. I don't know if such a book
exists (I doubt it). A highly specialized book like that, which
would be so useful, justifies the combinatory fable of the mon-
key infinitely typing at random. It's a "possible" book like any

other, but expecting chance to produce it is just too much of a stretch: various infinities would have to be aligned. Not to mention the fact that for me to understand it, there would have to be diagrams.

When people talk about astronomy, sooner or later they end up mentioning primitive cultures. In other disciplines too, but in astronomy it's an obsession. If we took these comments seriously, we'd have to believe that primitive people came up with the most ridiculous ideas about how the stars and planets move, and about nature in general. The supreme and most outrageous example is the idea that when the sun goes down at night, it will never come up again. With the most deeply rooted conviction, I maintain that this is false: there are no primitive peoples, there are no savages, or if we want to use those words to name other civilizations, we have no right to suppose that they are any less intelligent than we presume to be. There have always been stupid, gullible, ignorant people, and there is no shortage of them in our civilization. But a culture, be it that of naked jungle dwellers, has and always had all the knowledge that any other culture had or will have. My position on this is unyielding and militant. I believe that the error, encouraged by a latent racism, even among the most scrupulously right-thinking people, comes from a mistake in translation, or more precisely, a half translation, which isn't really a translation at all. Let's suppose that the people of a certain nation notice that the moon's recurring phases can be used to measure a certain lapse of time (what we call a "month") and, reasonably economizing their linguistic resources, they use the same word for that lapse and the moon (we do similar things). Now, somebody translating from their language is bound to write "Five moons ago" (when what the person really said was "Five months ago") without stopping to think that the same signifier is used for two different signifieds and that the identity between them is merely etymological or genealogical. That's how the Indians in ethnological studies, and later on in novels and films, end up saying: "Five moons no raining..." (since the idea is to make them sound stupid, they're not allowed to conjugate verbs either).

This example, apart from the fact that it's not really an example, is simplistic, but it gives an idea of what I'm getting at. A proper translation is a complete translation. In their language, the Indians say: "It hasn't rained for five months," exactly as we would. And when they speak of astronomy, medicine, love or whatever, they speak just as we would, except in their language, as we do in ours. To suppose anything else is an error, however it may gratify our desire to look down on them. Although the expression doesn't exactly capture my idea, you could say that I'm using an "extended concept of translation."

The same logic and the same implicit racism underlie appeals to the notion of "belief." The most absurd beliefs are always attributed to primitive people of all kinds: that a great snake drank a river, that the souls of the dead travel in a boat, whatever. It's more or less the same as saying that we "believe" our jokes. Here too it could be pointed out that there are stupid and ignorant people everywhere, but it's not that simple.

"Belief" is shorthand for the acceptance of certain signifying practices, without which society could not continue to function. A catalogue of everything that we believe, left untranslated, would make us look stupid too.

If I had to nominate my favorite lapse of time, the one I find most practical for organizing my life, it would be the week. Today is my last day in Pringles, a Thursday. I came last Thursday and I'm leaving today. I have come to the café to write, as usual. The blonde girl hasn't been here since the first day. I haven't seen her again. Since she told me that she doesn't live in Pringles, I initially assumed that she came on Thursday and stayed for the weekend, which is when the café must be busiest. When I didn't see her on Friday, I adopted a new hypothesis, supposing that she worked from Monday to Thursday ... But that turned out to be wrong too. Maybe she doesn't work here anymore. Maybe she works certain days in the month, and my week-based reasoning is inapplicable. There are a thousand possibilities. The lives of strangers have their own rules, which differ from case to case, and anyone who tries to deduce them from a chance meeting is bound to get lost in an ocean of conjectures. It's strange to think that even the most predictable creature of habit, like myself, might, from a stranger's point of view, appear and disappear in an apparently random fashion. Tonight, for example, I'm leaving Pringles and I won't be back for several months.

There's so much we don't know! Before coming to Pringles, I had begun to wonder about the things I thought I knew but didn't really know at all—I must have been following a train of thought prompted by that business with the moon, although I didn't consciously make the connection. By some association of ideas, it had occurred to me that perhaps I could fill those gaps. I allowed a number of modest but time-honored puzzles to float up at random to the surface of my mind, without making any kind of selection. The first was this: if a circle turns, is it true that the central point remains still? The initial, irresistible impulse is to say: of course! It seems natural. But it should be the other way around; it should seem more natural for the central point to turn as well, like a miniature circle. Some kind of cultural aberration has intervened, and it has become a conditioned reflex to say that the central point is immobile almost as if that guaranteed the movement of the rest of the circle.

I pondered this for several days. Little by little, I turned my mind toward the inconceivable. I could imagine a nail hammered into the center of a circle: the nail stays still and the circle turns around it. But in that case the supposed point is not actually a part of the circle, so it's irrelevant to the problem. In the end, I asked Tomasito, with a certain apprehension, because my son is a bit of a grouch.

"Of course!" he replied. "The central point doesn't turn."

"But don't you think that the point, however small, is a little circle too, which has to turn along with the rest?"

"If it was a physical point, sure. But we're talking about a mathematical point."

I didn't pursue the matter. Fine. I didn't want to exasperate him.

A mathematical point? What is that? If it's a mental construction, why postulate it? Reality is complicated enough already; why burden it with pedantic fictions? The only function I can think of for that fixed point is keeping the circle in place. And who said the circle has to stay in the same place? Anyway, even if it stays in its place on a table, it's still moving because the earth is turning, etc. It could even be argued that circles are always still, and when they seem to be spinning it's because the world is turning around them.

That night, on my regular walk, I came to a definitive conclusion: there is no still point at the center, because if there was, it would lock the circle in place and stop it from turning. That's where I dug in my heels. To me, it was clear as day. I know it must be a ridiculous error, but it's one that I'm prepared to live and die with.

How we change! I used to scorn people who reasoned in this "Robinson Crusoe" way. I saw it as the epitome of ignorance, the mark of stubborn, self-satisfied fools, who act as if there were no books, as if knowledge began and ended in their vacuous heads. At the height of my extremism, I even regarded simply thinking for oneself as a form of obscurantism. It's what I still believe, in fact: knowledge is out there in books, not in what you can dream up on your own. People who think deserve their mistakes. And here I am, doing this pathetic intellectual handiwork ...

Anyway, tonight I'm off. Time to go. My weeks in Pringles

follow a strict pattern; or not so strict, actually, because they consist of a week and a day. The prospect of a long night sitting on the Estrella bus always makes me slightly anxious. Especially before the return trip to Buenos Aires because I won't get a minute's sleep. I suppose there is a remote chance of nodding off, but even before I get on the bus I'm resigned to staying awake.

I've done the trip dozens of times in recent years and in spite of my absentmindedness, there's something I couldn't help noticing: I sleep on the way down to Pringles but never on the way back. If it didn't have such an effect on me (that sleepless night is genuine torture, and I'm a wreck the following day), I might have gone back and forth thousands of times without becoming aware of the pattern, but what really brought it home was being politely asked, at one end of the trip or the other, Did you get any sleep? Since noticing, I have examined all the circumstances of each trip, to see if I can single out the one that is responsible for my insomnia: what I ate for dinner, the clothes I was wearing, where I was seated, my posture ... I even factored in my expectations: the contrasting psychological states of the outward-bound and the homeward-bound traveler. But it's futile: there don't seem to be any circumstantial causes. Which leaves only the direction: southward on the way there, northward on the way back. And this may oblige me to reconsider my conviction that the adepts of Feng Shui, terrestrial magnetism, and so on have all been taken in by charlatans. My skepticism has suffered so many blows, one more could bring it tumbling down. For the moment, though, it's holding out.

"Pringles, city of scented taxis." When I arrive at dawn and open the door of one of the taxis waiting in front of the bus terminal, I'm nauseated by the overpowering scent. The town's taxi drivers, who form a highly organized guild, scent their vehicles with various kinds of air freshener, and emulation or habituation have led them from use to abuse. In a way, it's understandable. These taxi drivers were once smallholders, pushed off the land by economic concentration and the expansion of agribusiness, and they have invested the money from the sale of their land in precious European or Japanese cars, which they use as taxis and cherish like favorite children. Behind the wheel, their hefty laborer's bodies are graced with a miraculous delicacy and precision, and their big paw-like hands dance lightly over the buttons of the electronic dashboard. They haven't had to change their habits all that much: they're still getting up before dawn, now to fetch travelers from the terminal, and in their obliging customer service, these former lords of the lonely pampas display the finest flowers of adaptation. The cars gleam outside and in. For the drivers, the scent must be a supreme and necessary elegance.

The desolation of Pringles, especially in winter, makes it seem an abstract place. If I had the time and the inclination, I would go through all the philosophical systems, from Plato to Nietzsche, and submit them to the Pringles test, measuring their claims against the absoluteness of the town. "Essence precedes existence," yes, all right, everywhere except in Pringles, where existence precedes essence, or the two go hand in hand. "To be is to be perceived": true, as shown by observation in Pringles. Etc.

VI

LIKE ALL OF MY CONTEMPORARIES, I COULD DIE AT ANY
moment. Today, tomorrow, yesterday. An accident, or a fatal ill-
ness (it wouldn't be all that unusual, at my age) ... It's a lottery,
but luckily it seems to be as difficult to win (or to lose, in this
case) as a real lottery with tickets. What I would feel, if it happened to me, was that an injustice had been done, or even that
some mistake had been made. How can I die if I haven't even
lived yet? Believers console themselves with the idea of "the
life to come," the happy life of the blessed, especially in cases
of premature death. Naturally, that was how the girl at the Avenida thought about her brother. I would find it much harder to
apply that idea to myself, because the very concept of a life "to
come" presupposes a life "here and now." If you haven't lived
even one life, what's the point of starting over? You might say
that everyone has a life, no matter how brief. But that kind of
simplification implies that there is equal cause to lament the
death of a five-year-old child and that of a man of ninety. It's
conventional sentimentalism. The lamenting is always done by

other people, who don't really care at all, at least compared to the way they would care about their own deaths. To lament, you have to be alive, which almost always means you're waiting for life to begin.

In a way, you don't have to be a believer to believe in the life to come, because the two lives are superimposed and blended in the present. "He who waits despairs," as the proverb says. I would say: "He who waits deludes himself" because what you're waiting for has already begun and sometimes it's already over. That's the nature of the present.

Last night before falling asleep, I was trying to clarify the question of the Last Judgment. According to my simplified version of Christian eschatology, the dead have to wait for the Last Judgment to be judged and assigned a definitive destiny in the life to come. You die, and then there's a blank space, a nothing, until you wake up on Judgment Day. The living, that is, the survivors, might imagine that the dead go directly to Heaven or Hell, but it can't be like that for the dead themselves, because there would have to be two times running simultaneously— Eternity and time in the world—and that is impossible. So we have to wait until the end of time, till Judgment; all the rest (simultaneity, Dante, the return of the living dead, spiritualism, and so on) falls into the category of fiction. There's another reason too: people can't be definitively judged at the moment of their death, because they go on affecting the present via the continuing reverberation of their deeds and works, or simply

because of the weight they had in the system of the world, be it
great or small, which means that they go on accumulating merits and demerits. Logic dictates that this action will continue
for as long as there is time, so a just evaluation has to wait until
time comes to an end.

But this leap from death to the Last Judgment poses a number of problems. Last night I got so tangled in my calculations
I couldn't get to sleep; I was tempted to get up and draw a dia-
gram to see if I could set it out clearly. Maybe I can do that
now.

Consider a man who dies on the fifth of June 1932 at ten min-
utes past ten in the morning; from that point on, there's a blank,
until the Last Judgment, whenever that happens to be. Since
his consciousness has been extinguished by death, to him that
blank can only be an instant, even if it lasts ten thousand cen-
turies. If we were to think of it as a lapse of time, like a kind of
dark waiting room, that would be *another* "life to come," a third
life, which seems a little excessive to me. As far as I know, no
one has ever spoken of a third, intermediate life. I am familiar
with the notion of "Limbo," but I don't think it's accepted by serious theologians; it must be a fictional compromise, invented
to make the ideas of immediate judgment and instantaneous
Heaven and Hell fit with the requirements of dogma. And it's a
dangerous fiction, because it could lead evildoers to speculate
about the time to be served.

An instant, then. You close your eyes, or they fall shut, and you open them again immediately on the day and at the very hour of time's completion. In other words, for the man in our example, the Last Judgment took place on the fifth of July 1932 at ten past ten in the morning.

But a minute later, there was another death (I say a minute but it could be half a minute or two seconds: it depends on the mortality rate, which must vary anyway) and a minute before, there had been another, and so on, forwards and backwards, all through History. And with each death, the same thing happens, that is, there is the same kind of leap, whose duration is variable from an external perspective, but always the same — zero — from the point of view of the person concerned.

And that's what makes this figure so hard to conceive. There is a set with multiple members (human beings) whose deaths progressively punctuate the full range of time, yet the end of the range is present at each one of those points. The end of time is contiguous with every one of its moments.

As I said, you don't have to be a Christian, or hold particular beliefs, for these things to apply. They can be generalized to all situations that involve the individual and the collective. The bridge between those two registers is made of interruptions and leaps. You only have to think of all the people who are sleeping on the planet and those who are awake: there are millions of minuscule Last Judgments spread out to form an enormous, complicated figure. And it doesn't even have to be an interruption of consciousness, because any kind of waiting performs the same function. While some people are waiting for things to happen, others are living, and then the roles are reversed, and this alternation is what time comes down to, in practice.

VII

IN THE FABLE OF THE LAST JUDGMENT, EACH PERSON falls asleep separately and everyone wakes up together. The great event is a *terminus ad quem* from which the innumerable range of individuals can be viewed; when they come together in that knot, their individuality is revealed, and they must pay for it. But that event is unique, unrepeatable and maximally deferred; in fact, deferral as a secondary event is defined by reference to the Last Judgment, which is the model of all waiting.

Each individual life reproduces the model in miniature. Or rather, since the Last Judgment is actually a fiction, its purpose is to provide a model for our daily manipulation of time and to make it intelligible. In real life, we fall asleep separately ("Blessed are the sleepy ones, for they shall soon fall off": Nietzsche) and we wake up separately too. That's the catch: we wake up separately, according to our rhythms or necessities or whims … but we wake up to reality, which is a great collective event in which everyone participates.

I'm not referring only to literal sleeping, but to any kind of absence, like a vacation at the beach, or a term in jail, and I'm thinking especially of states of distraction or absorption or partial blindness ... categories that cover almost everything: life is made of these absences.

We're always coming back. And while we were away, things happened. We emerge from sleep to observe their effects, like Rip Van Winkle.

And that's just it: I feel like Rip Van Winkle. That's what I was trying to get to. Today, the fifth of July 1999, I wake and pick up the thread of my thoughts where I left it thirty years ago. This sounds like a metaphor, and perhaps it is, but it should also be understood literally. Suddenly it hits you: you're not twenty; you're not young any more ... and in the meantime, while you were thinking about something else, the world has changed. The succession of my ideas was interrupted, and now it's hard for me to resume it, because those ideas no longer correspond to anything objective, which means that they're not really ideas. I want to be completely sincere about this, but to tell the truth I no longer know if I'm thinking or raving. I guess this is what always happens: the collective, world politics, is the hardest thing to grasp in thought, because it has so many facets. Nevertheless, one of the ideas that implanted itself in my young mind was the indignity of work in a capitalist society. Now I don't know what to do with that idea, because the masses are clamoring precisely for work, and the right-minded, to whose ranks I thought I belonged, are praising it to the skies,

as if it were a panacea. I was convinced that the oppressed had
nothing to lose but their chains, and here they are demanding
them desperately.

This doesn't necessarily mean that the world has been
turned upside down; in fact, it has simply regressed to an ear-
lier stage of the same situation. Which means that we, the bour-
geoisie, have executed a clever maneuver and claimed a victory
by making time run backwards, which gives us an extra century
or two in which to come up with new maneuvers and secure
new victories.

The whole idea of the Revolution, with which we were so
taken up, was premised on the unspoken assumption that a
century or two would have to pass. Deep down, we knew this.
The contradictions could not be resolved *in situ*, in our lives.
We were working for the future, not the present. The present
fell into a gap.

When you committed yourself to the Revolution, you re-
nounced your chronological autonomy and put yourself at the
mercy of delays that were out of your control. You threw yourself into a temporal abyss. Your own personal death became the
guarantee of the whole operation because it was required for
the extinction of your class, your kind, your world.

The reason for my perplexity is this: the results that are plain
to see were obtained in a few decades, within a single genera-
tion, and the people involved are the same, except that where
they used to say *white* now they're saying *black*. It's a different

world, a world turned upside down, but with the same inhabitants. While I was absent (where?), they went on living.

They are still my contemporaries. Humanity is still my exact contemporary. But they think the exact opposite of what they were thinking when I left them, thirty years or half an hour ago, and they don't seem at all surprised by the change; they haven't even noticed it. They behave in a perfectly natural way, magically adapted to the world. And that, I realize, is the key to effective thinking: naturalness, spontaneity. It doesn't have to be thought out; it just happens by force of circumstance, like rain.

The transvaluation of work is one of the many things that amaze me. Another is the de-Machiavellization of state-level politics. Suddenly people have started judging the state by the norms of private virtue, honesty above all. The same honesty that is threatened when the proletariat is stripped of work. Public virtues (*la virtù*) have dissolved. This, I suppose, is due to the fact that public matters are now decided by corporations, and the only function left to the state is that of providing a model of ethical perfection, like the court in imperial China. But there's no point in giving examples, because I'm talking about what actually happened, not what it might exemplify. "If you don't believe me, go and see for yourself" (Lautréamont).

If it was a matter of giving examples, nothing more would be required. The other day I read in the paper that somewhere in Africa (the Sudan, I think), slavery has survived, and proletarians old enough to work are sold for fifty dollars. A Swiss humanitarian organization collected money, "bought" two thousand slaves and set them free. It didn't cost them very much (a hundred thousand dollars) but it gave them a godlike status; there was a photo of the ex-slaves, sitting on the ground, looking disconcerted and not very happy. In some ways their situation is similar to ours today. "Slavery" is a word, which in this case seems to have been applied to an ancestral tradition. It's not unreasonable to suppose that there is a kind of traditional contract by which people sell their work in return for board and lodging, and possibly clothes and other benefits. Is that so different from what our unemployed are demanding? If the African contract includes restrictions on movement or change of employment, those restrictions have their equivalents in our "civilized" contracts, or they are counterbalanced by stability. Or they simply don't matter, if the alternative is starving to death.

Let's suppose that a Swiss humanitarian organization discovers that Argentine proletarians are working twelve or fourteen hours a day, for a salary that doesn't even cover basic necessities, in conditions that they judge to be unfit for humans, etc. From their Swiss point of view, they could well call that "slavery" and, spurred by a feeling of just indignation, collect money to "buy out" the contracts of two thousand or twenty thousand exploited Argentines and give them back their "freedom." There in Zurich, or in Basel, they wouldn't know that those same Argentines had spent years marching and blocking traffic to demand "work" ...

The moral is that each country still defines its words autonomously, as it did before globalization. And trying to impose a definition on others, even with the best intentions, can be catastrophic.

Of course I didn't spend the last thirty years napping; I spent them writing my little novels and preparing my Encyclopedia. The fact that I was also reading the newspaper every day is immaterial, it seems. The whole purpose of writing was to dissolve the exemplary quality of my "impressions of Africa," to make them historical, and articulate within them the two contradictory aspects of the world: identity and difference. By writing, I've managed to stay alive until now, to stay, that is, in the same world; the price I've had to pay is that it has turned upside down.

It's true that I could be condemned for not having used my privileges as a bourgeois intellectual to do something more constructive, if only at the individual level, like becoming more learned or intelligent, or at least writing truly good books. But what's the point of writing good books, or learning, or discovering new truths? Contributing to the construction and accumulation of knowledge means collaborating with power, since power will inevitably appropriate that knowledge and exploit it to dominate and subjugate. So what should you do? Keep the knowledge secret? Use it first, for revolutionary purposes? (But knowing what comes first and what comes after is no simple matter in this domain.) As a precautionary measure, I persisted in the most complete stupidity.

And anyway, I never believed that knowing things was worth the trouble. It never seemed worth the effort to me, in practical terms.

I have always let information flow through my head like water through a hose.

After all, I knew where the facts were and I could go and fetch them if I ever needed to, but frankly I never thought it would come to that. As I saw it, this was the only practical benefit of my favorite pastime, reading: it showed me how to find the facts should I ever be required to put them to some use, an event that this preparation rendered all the more unlikely.

What interested me was something else, something more aesthetic: the format of the information and how it was constructed. That was what stayed with me, without any exercise of memory on my part. All my attention was focused on the format; there was none left over for the rest. I don't know if my memory withered away through lack of use or if it was always poor; what I do know is that my mind has remained pure of content. This explains why I'm so inept in conversations: I don't have anything to say, I have lost touch with content.

VIII

I USED TO WRITE WITH THE SOLE AIM OF PRODUCING work of high quality: good novels, better than others, etc. The reasons for wanting to do this are psychological; in other words, they can be found somewhere in a vast and ill-defined jumble that offers something to satisfy every taste: ambition, adaptation, inferiority complex, megalomania, compensation ... Good arguments could be found for each of these hypotheses, and I find them myself, in my meditations. But the only thing I know for sure is that my aim in writing was to do it well and become a good writer, which was all that mattered to me. As opposed to most decisions in the life of an individual, which are determined by an innumerable variety of causes, this aim of mine was something of an *idée fixe*. Not that I think it was "mine" exclusively; the general idea must be common enough, though perhaps not universally shared. You want to do something well, so you sacrifice everything else to that objective, obscurely aware that once it is attained, everything else will be thrown in for free. Excuses will always be found for a good writer; for a bad one, no excuse is valid.

Anyway, at a certain point, having published about twenty books, I had to get down to some serious thinking. You can't go on learning indefinitely, whatever people say. I mean, it's true that you go on learning, but bad habits also become more deeply ingrained, and the bad offsets the good. Hoping starts to lose its pertinence: the true object of hope is always something new; even those who want to go back to the past are imagining a new past. In literature above all, the good is identified with the new; but I think that in my most lucid moments what I wanted to write was not so much something good as something new, something that had never been written before. And the new is subject to the law of diminishing returns, which I revere. What didn't work out on a first attempt is less and less likely to work out.

Also, after the happy recklessness of youth, when things get done, if they do, in spite of the doer's aspirations, it's counterproductive to persist in striving for quality. I have always subscribed to the idea of High or Highbrow Culture, Art with a capital *A*. And art is not something that should be done well. If doing it well is what counts, it's craft, production for sale, and therefore subject to the taste of the buyer, who will naturally want something good. But art creates its own paradigm. It isn't "good" according to preexisting standards; rather, it sets the standard for what is to come (the crafts of the future). That's the difference between creation and production.

So what happened five or six years ago is that I began, in a

typically defensive way, to distance myself from the old habits
of my youth. I began to shift the focus of my attention to a totalizing project for which my literary works would serve as preparatory steps, advertisements and teasers. I came to think of my
little novels, which I went on writing—partly out of habit and
partly to perfect my alibi—as marginal documentation, and
the process of writing them as a means of understanding my
life. The life of the author of the Encyclopedia.

Because that is the key name for this grand project: the Encyclopedia. And that's what it is, too: a kind of general com-
pendium, containing everything. The aim of a whole life is to
acquire the whole of knowledge. The final record of that quest
is the Encyclopedia.

I have a big folder full of preliminary notes, on which I work
intermittently. It's clear from the totalizing premises that this
is one of those infinite projects whose completion date is irrelevant because it can't actually be completed. Which is ideal for
me. It allows me to rest. I have spent my life rushing to finish
tasks, so as to be able to die in peace; but the Encyclopedia in-
corporates my death as a "glorious failure," so I can go on writing as I please without having to worry at all.

The first novelty of my Encyclopedia is that it will be the
work of a single person. The second is that it will not be lim-
ited to the general but venture into the particular. All encyclo-
pedias do this, in as much as they include historical facts; mine
will also treat the general as so many particular cases, because a

generality is always a construction, so it too is a historical fact, anchored in a time and a place. The third novelty is a complicated game of equivalences, ensuring that each cultural-historical complex includes all the others, in varying forms but always reconstructing the same system of functions. Thus each particularity can subsist without the support of generalization. But enough. I'm in no rush to explain myself here, because it's all in that big file of notes. I'm not going to end up having to scribble "I've run out of time" in the margin; I made sure of that from the start.

What I have in the file, of course, are sketches, plans and programs, the theory of the Encyclopedia; I haven't written a single page of the text itself. By this stage, I wouldn't know where to begin. The further I advance in the epistemological prolegomena, the further I leave the actual beginning behind. The genre of "preparatory notes" has its own aesthetic, its own kind of finish, and I'm becoming more susceptible to its charms as I reread Mallarmé's notes for *Le Livre* and Duchamp's for *The Large Glass* and the notes that Novalis made for his encyclopedia ... Given the premises of my project, the only particular case that I could begin to write about is my own. I am the point at which the particular is particularized and the historical historicized. The sum of knowledge reverts to the individual, in his role as author of the Encyclopedia.

This question of particularities is really very literary. In a novel or a poem, it's not a matter of clothing particulars in generality (not even Lukacs with his theory of "types" was claiming that) but of making particularity absolute, so that the absolute stands in for the general. There is something impossible or insoluble here, and in order to set it out in black and white new forms must be sought. Those forms are what I've been searching for more or less inadvertently in my little novels, and if I think about it like that I don't feel so depressed about them. Let me see if I can explain myself: it's not a matter of using scientific laws to illuminate the figure of Napoleon; it's more like that old joke about the museum guide who shows some visitors a skull in a glass case: "This is the skull of Napoleon," and then when they get to another glass case in which there is a tiny skull: "And this is the skull of Napoleon when he was a child." It's a weary old joke, I know, but it must have been fresh once. Definitions of the joke always imply some kind of formal invention, which is new by its very nature. Everything new becomes old, that's an inescapable law. But the whole point here is to overcome laws that are universally valid. The new is preserved within the old, like the skull of the boy Napoleon inside the skull of the adult. This little joke, a modest mini-artwork accessible to everyone, conserves its cheerful novelty in spite of the tiresome repetitions, as something conceivable. It is also conceivable that every particular thing in the universe could be the object of a formal invention: iridescent, surprising, funny, unpredictable, like a butterfly with strange wing patterns flittering through a garden. In that sense my encyclopedia will be a recreative work.

All this is well and good for someone who has eternities of free time (especially in the afternoons) to spend sitting in cafés, playing the philosopher, pursuing daydreams that began in reading, and filling notebooks with futile jottings on this and that. Pastime, self-deception and excuse, in equal parts. An excuse, because it allows me to justify my unjustifiable novels as provisional approximations to a Great Work to come, to be realized on the far side of time. But like everyone else, I do occasionally have moments of candid self-appraisal. Involuntarily, but it happens, as with that wretched gaffe about the moon.

All right, then: I know nothing. Worse: I don't know anything. "All I know is I don't know it all." And I don't even have that knowledge in the form of a conviction; it's something I have to stumble over by accident. I'd rather not lapse into psychology, but even without the help of that discipline it's clear there's a hole in the much-touted totality. There's a hole in me, and in that little white darkness, I discover the real heart of the mystery, which is also my Rosetta Stone. If I could translate what I don't know into what I know, I would be able to understand the purpose of my life. As things are, it all seems an illusion, a simulacrum made of words. And even if I understood, the scandal of my ignorance would remain intact. I lean over this bottomless well, Narcissus reborn, and an unfamiliar sadness overcomes me. I think this is the first time I have felt like a part of humanity, just when I finally have a reason to feel different.

A particular fact should never be an "example" of something

general. Everyone accepts that "examples" serve as a natural hinge between the particular and the general. They proliferate in everyday speech, obviating the need for concepts, which are taken for granted. We're always using examples in explanations; it's almost inevitable, and we end up thinking that every particular is an example of something else, the thing we need to know about. In fact, "example" and "particular case" function as synonyms. The example, which was originally a rhetorical device, for use in persuasion, has become a way of conceiving the world, and this, in my opinion, diminishes the realness of reality. My Encyclopedia, if I were to write it, would be the central battlefield in a war against the aberrant logic of the example.

For all its merits, Wittgenstein's *Philosophical Investigations* is invalidated, I believe, by a blind acceptance of the exemplary function. The same applies to the work of almost all linguists; in fact, it's hard even to imagine a book on any aspect of language that would address the thing itself, rather than examples of it. That's why I prefer philology.

I began this book with something like an example: my ignorance about the phases of the moon and the alarm bell that it set off in my mind. As if to confirm the saying "Fear is a bad counselor," the alarm made this episode exemplary, interchangeable with any one of the many gaps in my knowledge, and then gave way to fatalism: it would be impossible to enumerate all my lacks, and yet by mentioning just one I could give an adequate idea of their general nature, and save ink. But I like to think that this anecdote is, in fact, the example of an example, which brings us full circle, to the thing itself, exemplifying nothing, pure historical reality: my life seen from the brink of death.

IX

HERE'S A STORY THAT I FIND THOUGHT-PROVOKING:
the death of Évariste Galois, at the age of twenty, in 1832. One
night, in a tavern, some loudmouths, who may have been put
up to it, provoked him into an argument over a woman, which
he was obliged to settle in a duel, to be fought the following
day, at dawn. He went to his room and spent the intervening
hours writing feverishly, in order to leave a record of his revolutionary mathematical discoveries. At first light he presented
himself on the field of honor and was killed. His work had been
written in one night, and it is work of great importance, fundamental to modern mathematics. It's a sad story, but in a way it
has a happy ending, because he was able to leave a testimony
of his genius, so he didn't live in vain. He was able to do this in
a few hours and in the space of a few pages. A novelist, in the
same circumstances, would have been doomed to failure. Galois could do it because he was a mathematician: mathematical notation made it possible. That was the key to his success,
I think. I have wasted many years, all the years of my youth,
searching for a system of literary notation; in other words, I

have spent the time granted by my futile survival imagining the instant of my untimely death.

I was searching for a system that would allow me to write all my novels on the last night. For Galois, the equivalent of this fantasy would have been to spend those nocturnal hours coming up with an infallible method for shooting accurately and surviving the duel. I think that's what I would have done in his place, since there can be no doubt that, in his place, I would have been a genius, so the attempt would not have been absurd. He was more sensible; he was a genius, but only in the domain of mathematics; trying to extend or extrapolate from that domain was a waste of time. But it's what I would have done, because I have entrusted my destiny to just that sort of maneuver: extensions and extrapolations, sometimes of the most fantastic kind. That's what literature is, as I understand it: extending and extrapolating meanings into the domain of the real. Galois's impeccable common sense told him that mathematics was one thing and reality quite another, and he stuck to mathematics.

Perhaps he had learned from his experience, which, although brief, had abounded in disasters. The tragic story of his father must have left its mark on him. Nicolas Gabriel Galois was a typical product of the Enlightenment. A Voltairean, an Encyclopedist and staunchly anticlerical, he was a fervent supporter of the Revolution and a faithful follower of Napoleon. During the last years of the Empire, he was the mayor of Bourg-la-Reine, the town near Paris where his son was born. A courteous and witty man with typically old-fashioned manners, he was well liked by the people of the town. His most notable skill was in versification: he could and habitually did come up with the most ingenious and charming rhymes about local events and characters. It is tempting to think that this rather frivolous talent was the core of the genetic heritage that he transmitted to his son; rhymes are linguistic equations, and we should not forget that it was in the field of algebraic equations that Évariste made one his most important discoveries. Versification, however, led to the downfall of his father. It is no secret that priests are unforgiving; they are also relentless and determined. A cunning village priest wrote a poem in the style of Nicolas Galois, full of obscene calumnies (or truths — it makes no difference) about the family of a prominent community member and circulated it under the name of the amiable poet. Now Galois senior should have foreseen an attack from that quarter, given the perfidy of the church, and should have been well equipped to resist, thanks to his philosophical education, but he fell apart, no doubt because the blow had found his weakest spot. This trick robbed him of the reason that he so revered. Rather than loss of face, the root cause of the breakdown must have been the theft of his style, which is everything in poetry. The mere idea that his harmless eccentricity might be misattributed was more than he could bear. He developed a virulent paranoia and killed himself soon after.

For his son, who was seventeen at the time, this tragedy was the confirmation of a kind of objective paranoia which expanded in concentric circles only to contract again. Even at that age, he had opened up whole new fields in mathematics, in spite of which he went on receiving low marks in a mediocre Catholic school. He had already failed the entrance examination for the École Polytechnique and would later be rejected again. These two failures have intrigued historians. The École Polytechnique was one of the finest in Europe at the time and its teaching staff were well trained and up-to-date in their knowledge, capable of recognizing scientific talent at first sight. Nor were there political or religious prejudices that might have intervened, because the establishment was a liberal and even subversive stronghold. How could they have failed the greatest living mathematician in an entrance exam, not once but twice? A plausible enough explanation combines factors of various kinds. In the first place, as a general rule, professors marking an exam take it for granted that they know more than the students: when the opposite occurs, the result is a dialogue of the deaf, even if there's no ill will. There was also a more particular reason: the young genius had acquired the habit of executing all the intermediate steps in his head and thus arriving abruptly at the results. At a certain level in mathematics, results matter far less than how they were produced, and it is performance at that level, precisely, that entrance examinations are designed to test. To make things worse, the examinations were oral.

Galois tried to make his discoveries public on three occasions. In 1829, a first memoir was submitted to the most renowned French mathematician of the day, Augustin-Louis Cauchy, who promised to present it to the Academy, but forgot to, didn't read the document and then lost it. The second and more important memoir, written as an entry for the Academy of Science's Grand Prize in Mathematics, was in fact presented; one of the judges took it home, but promptly died, and the manuscript disappeared among the rest of his papers. The third memoir, on the numerical resolution of equations, was presented to the Academy in 1831 and read, finally, by a prestigious mathematician, S. D. Poisson, who rejected it with the bald verdict: "Incomprehensible." Here the blame seems to lie with the elliptical style that had been the cause of Galois's failure in the oral exams, this time in writing. Joseph Liouville, the editor of his posthumous manuscripts, published in the *Journal des Mathématiques Pures et Appliquées* in 1846, attributes his "obscurity" to "an excessive desire for concision."

In any case, renouncing scientific glory, Galois threw himself into the political struggle, which he took to be the most effective means of destroying everything as soon as possible. There was no more ardent republican, no one more revolted by the Bourbon restoration, the divine right of kings and the power of the church. A pair of incendiary letters to a newspaper in the turbulent days of the 1830 revolution earned him a reputation as an extremist. At a republican banquet on the ninth of May 1831, he surprised his fellow diners with a toast to the king: "To Louis-Philippe ..." But looking more closely, they saw that he was holding an open jackknife, its glinting blade intended for the monarch's throat. As bad luck would have it, just at that moment, Alexandre Dumas, author of *The Three*

Musketeers and eminent informer, was passing the restaurant and witnessed this scene through the window. As a result, the police came looking for Galois and charged him with incitation to regicide. The lawyer hired by his friends had the good idea of arguing that the jackknife had been open in the diner's hand for the simple reason that he had been using it to cut the meat, a perfectly reasonable thing to be doing in a restaurant. The jury, moved to pity by the defendant's youth, made use of this accommodating fiction to acquit him.

But the police had no time for fictions; a few days later they arrested him again and accused him of illegally wearing a uniform (Galois had, in effect, although perhaps for want of other clothing, worn a part of the uniform of the Artillery Corps, into which he had been temporarily enlisted and which had since been disbanded by royal decree). This time he was held for six months without trial and released on bail only because cholera broke out in the prison, which had to be evacuated. A few weeks later, on the 29th of May 1832, the incident in the tavern occurred.

So that night, between the 29th and the 30th of May, he wrote it all down. As well as the famous pages in which his mathematical discoveries were recorded, with the heartrending sentence — "I don't have time" — repeated between paragraphs, he wrote some letters and a political manifesto, which he entitled, "Letter to All Republicans." It isn't reproduced in the biographies, so I haven't read it, which is maybe just as well, because I don't see how a snotty-nosed twenty-year-old can know anything about politics.

It was a duel with pistols, at twenty-five paces. His opponents and the seconds went off and left him lying wounded (maybe they thought he was dead), and there he remained for several hours until somebody saw him. He was taken to a hospital, where he died the following day. In the meantime, he was identified and the family were informed. A younger brother went to see him, in tears. Galois said: "Don't cry. I need all my courage to die at the age of twenty."

What would it be like to be twenty? If I make an effort, I can imagine the vigor and the freshness, the beauty and the buoyancy of that age. But I see it as something remote, a mental construction, almost unreal. Something that happened two hundred years ago, in another world, and yet at the same time curiously close and intimate. A personal fantasy. I try to make it real by extrapolating from the young people I see in the street, but it's not the same.

I find it easier to think about it indirectly, via the film that could be made about the life of Évariste Galois. I'm surprised that it hasn't been made already, unless it has and I've missed it (or maybe someone has written one of those aberrations known as "fictionalized biographies," which work in the same way). They would have to use his last night as the frame narrative, and the bulk of the story would unfold in a series of flashbacks. It's a trite and weary device, but in this case it would have a deep meaning, because it would thematize the mechanism of condensation and expansion that ruled Galois's life and work. Like mathematical formulae, accidents (and bad luck in general) are atomic concentrations of experience, projected onto the screen of time.

But the protagonist of the film would be one of those pretty actors, who are typically thirty years old, in spite of their boyish faces. However well done, it would be a falsification. Real youth is something beyond the reach of images.

A young man still has to start living. He might have had all the ideas in the world, but he still has to revise, correct and invert them. That's why he needs all the following years and decades. The ideas can only serve as mnemonic devices. Having it all in your head, like Évariste addressing the professors, is a sign of youth. I have sometimes been tempted by the idea of a life lived straightaway, once and for all. But it's impossible, because you would have to die first.

X

YOU CAN'T WRITE A NOVEL THE NIGHT BEFORE DYING.
Not even one of the very short novels that I write. I could make
them shorter, but it still wouldn't work. The novel requires an
accumulation of time, a succession of different days: without
that, it isn't a novel. What has been written one day must be
affirmed the next, not by going back to correct it (which is futile) but by pressing on, supplying the sense that was lacking
by advancing resolutely. This seems magical, but in fact it's how
everything works; living, for a start. In this respect, which is
fundamental, the novel defeats the law of diminishing returns,
reformulating it and turning it to advantage.

This law, which I'm always referring to, can be explained in
the following way: imagine there's a steel spring, a yard high,
standing on the ground. We put a three-pound weight on it, and
it goes down thirty-two inches, so now the spring's just four
inches high, but to make it go down another inch, you have to
add a weight of three hundred pounds. And then to make it go
down another fraction of an inch, you have to pile on tons ...
The same thing happens in intellectual work, not because there

is some necessary relation between the intellectual and the physical, it just happens to happen—analogy wins out. Somebody opens up a new field of artistic or intellectual endeavor and in that initial impetus occupies it almost entirely. The classic case is Euclid: once he had the fundamental idea, he was able to complete his book within a few days, or perhaps a few hours, and geometry was done. In the two thousand years that followed, an innumerable legion of geometers, dedicating their whole lives to the field, could do no more than add a few superfluous details. This, of course, is not an example. It's what actually happened. The fact that something similar happened in other cases (Freud, Darwin) shows that the law of diminishing returns is valid, but doesn't reduce the protagonists to examples because each particular case is, by definition, a historical whole. That totality is reconstructed each time an artist discovers his or her style. To discover a style is to realize it, in a complete and finished form, and after that there's nothing left to do except to go on producing. Since artists generally reach this point while they're still young, they spend the rest of their lives in an atmosphere of futility and disquiet, if not outright anxiety in the face of what seems a colossal task, which would require ten lifetimes to complete, and even then would yield very meager fruit: compressing the spring another fraction of an inch, taking one more step after leaping a thousand leagues ...

I thought I had found a way out of this trap, a daily, livable solution, in the writing of novels, since they keep putting off the artistic consummation that serves to justify them. Kafka must have been thinking along these lines when he complained about interruptions and said that a story would spoil if he couldn't get the whole thing written in one sitting. But for him, writing novels was not a solution, because they became unfinishable. I solved the problem in my own way, by taking the fine art of botching to a new level. I was so bored and ashamed by what I was doing, I felt that I might as well die as soon as the novel was done, but not before, because no one else would know how to finish it. So I would rush on to the end, always arriving sooner than I'd expected (sacrificing quality, it's true), and then as a mark of relief, I would inscribe the date at the foot of the final page.

Not only is it impossible to write a novel the night before "the distinguished thing" (Henry James); in reality, in practice, novels are rarely written in the weeks or months or years leading up to it. Novelists tend to retire well before that. I did, a few years ago, although I have maintained a respectable semblance of activity. It happened gradually, and at first I didn't even notice that I was no longer writing novels. I wrote first chapters, gave up, set them aside for later, had a better idea ... And all that remained was a feeling of dissatisfaction and impotence.

Eventually I realized where the problem lay: in what has been called "the invention of circumstantial details," that is, precise notations concerning the place, the time, the characters, their clothes, their gestures, all the things that set the scene. It began to seem ridiculous and childish, this fussiness in the realm of fantasy, this information about things that don't really exist. But without circumstantial details you don't have a novel, or you do but it's abstract and disembodied, and what's the point of that? When I became aware of this block, I began to look for a solution, because I don't really want to give up writing, but I can't see any way around it. Perversely and predictably enough, the only plots that occur to me now require the abundant invention of circumstantial details. Faithful to my "flight-forward" procedure, I tried to turn the problem into a theme and write about it, but by its very nature this is one of the trickiest things to thematize.

Actually, I have nothing against circumstantial details. There's nothing wrong with them; on the contrary, I am grateful to them for the major part of my readerly pleasures over the years. They have always been used in the writing of novels, and I still admire good novels, as much as I ever did, or more. The author invents a character, and for that character to do things in the unfolding daydream of the novel, he has to walk down a street or sit in an armchair, enter a house, follow the flight of a fly, feel cold or hot; then a dog barks, or a rooster crows, the window is ajar, or wide open, or shut; the character's tie is ... green ... OK, OK. All that and much more. It has to be done, there's no alternative. But why does it have to be done *by me*? There's a reason why reading is more fun than writing. Why can't someone else do it? Why can't they have done it *already*? Circumstantial details are not so bad when you think of them as readymades. Once written down, they take on an air of necessity, almost like real things. But in the moment of inventing them, they're so childish, so silly ... Just thinking about it fills me with an invincible despondency.

What is to be done, then? "What is to be done?" (Lenin). That is what I spent my life doing; it's all I know how to do. And now I don't want to do it Maybe I should change direction, find a new activity. I've often thought about it; and perhaps this is the time to act, prompted by my aversion to one of the art's essential technicalities. But I really don't know how to do anything else, so if I stopped writing ... What would I do? Live? That's the classic answer. Which presupposes that I haven't been living up till now. "Living" would be what lies ineffably beyond all renunciations and relinquishments: illumination, the Grand Prize. But no, I can't believe that. It's ridiculous, an adolescent cliché. I can't believe I ever took it seriously, even for a second.

And yet the formula that I keep repeating to myself as incantation and talisman is: "I haven't lived." Really? What did I do then? What did I do in fifty years? I could draw up a fairly long list because, after all, I've done a lot, and yet I insist: I haven't lived. Thousands of things have happened to me, but not the things that should have happened. For example (except that it's not an example), I have never spoken with the dead, unlike the waitress in Pringles. That's why I can't hold up my end of a normal conversation. I have to keep quiet, listening to what the other person says, and later on, wandering around on my own in the labyrinths of my fantasy, I come up with something I might have said or done and promptly note it down, and then

I wedge it into the unfinished novel that I have conveniently at hand, whether it fits or not. That's where "circumstantial details" come from, basically. No wonder I've ended up loathing them.

I can't talk with a dead-brother-Jesus because I'm not a believer. I'm the sort of person who doesn't believe in anything. Which is nothing to be proud of because not believing is a sign of immaturity or inexperience. If things had happened to me, I would have no choice but to believe in them. Except that I'm a maximalist and I say: Even if I saw it with my own eyes, I wouldn't believe it. If the Virgin appeared to me in all her splendor, my disbelief would find a firm footing, and I would become a true unbeliever. This seems to me the only honest position, since to be skeptical in a provisional way, while waiting for a miracle, is the height of credulity.

I have been tested in this respect by a kind of miracle in reverse, a bad miracle: losing the two dearest friends of my adult life. Osvaldo and Jorgito died young: at forty-five and fifty-four respectively. In both cases, when it happened, I took refuge in the most intransigent denial. Under the illusion that they were still alive, I planned our reunions, imagined how we'd laugh at the misunderstanding ... This is a common reaction; it must be a natural defense mechanism. It takes a while to get used to the idea. "I can't believe it ..." Perhaps the sole purpose of belief in general is to prepare its own negation and thereby help us through hard times. But the thing is, I *still* don't believe it. I can't believe that Osvaldo is dead. I can't believe that Jorgito is dead. I just can't. I remember Osvaldo saying: "I can't believe that Perón has died." He must have come round to it in the end, because he was normal. And the waitress in Pringles said that she didn't believe in the death of her brother, but she was refusing to believe in one thing in order to believe in another, using her disbelief as a springboard. She was normal too, at least more normal than I am. In the end you believe in things because they have gone beyond the phase of their invention and actually occurred.

I once wrote, in all sincerity, that I take no measures to preserve my health or safety, because it isn't worth the trouble. To treat a life like mine as precious would be inelegant; or, to put it another way, the only elegant thing to do with such a life is to hold it in scorn, or at least to remain perfectly indifferent to its continuity or interruption. If I think about it, I have to conclude that there are two cases and only two in which I would look after myself: if I were a genius or a millionaire. Only then would I be able to do everything (in my hallucinations or in reality, respectively: either would be fine) and that would give me a reason to want what almost everybody wants: to go on living indefinitely, because to do everything, or anything at all, you have to be alive. By an amazing coincidence my two friends fulfilled those conditions, and I wonder now if that's why they were my friends: Osvaldo was a genius, Jorgito a millionaire. Literally, not metaphorically. They died, and I survived.

If I stopped writing, I would feel there was nothing left; it would be like demolishing a bridge that I haven't yet crossed.

If I go on living, I'll certainly go on writing. I'll work out some way to do it. But not if I die tomorrow. Tomorrow, of course, I'll have finished and dated this book. I'm hurrying to finish it today, rushing on blindly and deafly; the only thing that matters to me at this point is getting to the end, and actually there's nothing to stop me doing that right now.

If I had to sum up, I would formulate the problem like this: all my life I pursued knowledge, but I pursued it outside time, and time took its revenge by unfolding elsewhere. That's why experience taught me nothing (that business with the moon), and knowledge remained on the plane of hallucination. And now I find that even that plane is abandoning me, folding up and vanishing ... In a good novel the illusion is achieved by accumulating circumstantial details, which is a task that requires belief. You have to believe the day before you do it, and the following day, you have to have believed.

I say "day" because I'm immersed in this day, on which I will finish and date a book. And because death also happens on a particular day. I could say "years" or "decades." But my years and decades have already gone by. To write, you have to be young; to write well, you have to be a young prodigy. By the time you get to fifty, much of that energy and precision is gone.

JULY 18, 1999

PRAISE FOR CÉSAR AIRA

CONVERSATIONS

"Aira is able to develop a uniquely bogus set of facts that feels as realistic as waking up each morning and going to work, despite their fantastical and unrealistic qualities." – *Three Percent*

DINNER

"*Dinner* is far more intelligent than your average zombie tale, and more richly drawn" – Jessica Loudis, *TLS*

EMA, THE CAPTIVE

"*Ema* is as inventive and aphoristic as Aira's best works." – Alena Graedon, *The New Yorker*

"One of the Argentine master's oldest works, it's also one of his most memorable." – Juan Vidal, NPR Books

AN EPISODE IN THE LIFE OF A LANDSCAPE PAINTER

"Astonishing ... a supercharged Céline, writing with a Star Wars laser sword, turning Don Quixote into Picasso."   – *Harper's*

GHOSTS

"Exhilarating. César Aira is the Duchamp of Latin American literature.   – *The New York Times Book Review*

"Aira conjures a languorous, surreal atmosphere of baking heat and quietly menacing shadows that puts one in mind of a painting by de Chirico."   – *The New Yorker*

THE HARE

★ "Simultaneously an homage and deconstruction of the Victorian adventure story."   – *Publisher's Weekly*

HOW I BECAME A NUN

"*How I Became a Nun* is the work of an uncompromising literary trickster."   – *Time Out*

THE LINDEN TREE

"It has taken 14 years for this book to reach us in English, and that is too long to wait. We want more, and we want it yesterday."
– Patrick Flanery, *Spectator*

THE LITERARY CONFERENCE

"Aira's novels are eccentric clones of reality, where the lights are brighter, the picture is sharper and everything happens at the speed of thought."   – *The Millions*

THE LITTLE BUDDHIST MONK & THE PROOF

"Aira's blazing novelettes serve as a reminder (as "Proof") that there are some things that can only be pulled off in writing, and that these things can flare up and vanish in the space of 90 pages, leaving their beautiful, inexplicable ash swirling in our minds."
– Brenton Woodward, *Liminoid Magazine*

THE MIRACLE CURES OF DR. AIRA

"César Aira is indeed Dr. Aira, and the miracles are the little books he creates."   – *The Coffin Factory*

THE MUSICAL BRAIN

"Aira's stories seem like shards from an ever-expanding inter-connecting universe."   – Patti Smith, *The New York Times*

THE SEAMSTRESS AND THE WIND

"A beautiful, strange fable ... alternating between frivolity, insight, and horror."   – *Quarterly Conversation*

SHANTYTOWN

"With a few final acts of narrative sleight of hand (and some odd soliloquies) the reader is left at once dazzled and unsettled."
– *Los Angeles Times*

VARAMO

"Aira seems fascinated by the idea of storytelling as invention, invention as improvisation and improvisation as transgression, as *getting away with something*."   – *The New York Times Book Review*

"A lampoon of our need for narrative. No one these days does metafiction like Aira."   – *The Paris Review*